MISS BUNSEN'S SCHOOL FOR BRILLIANT GIRLS

Light as a Feather

MISS BUNSEN'S SCHOOL FOR BRILLIANT GIRLS

Light as a Feather

Erica-Jane Waters

Albert Whitman & Company
Chicago, Illinois

Library of Congress Cataloging-in-Publication data
is on file with the publisher.

Text and illustrations copyright © 2019 by Erica-Jane Waters
Hardcover edition first published in the United States of America
in 2019 by Albert Whitman & Company
Paperback edition first published in the United States of America
in 2020 by Albert Whitman & Company
ISBN 978-0-8075-5153-0 (paperback)
ISBN 978-0-8075-5155-4 (ebook)

Printed in the United States of America
10 9 8 7 6 5 4 3 2 1 LSC 24 23 22 21 20

Design by Ellen Kokontis

For more information about Albert Whitman & Company,
visit our website at www.albertwhitman.com.

For my brilliant girl,
Sienna-Rose

Chapter 1

"Go on, Pearl!" shouted Millie.

"Go on. Give it some!" cried Halinka.

Pearl elbowed her way through the other players, her specially improvised running shoes helping her fly across the field faster than a rocket as she guided the ball toward the goal. The cries and cheers from her fellow Bunseners in the sports arena faded to a dull murmur as her heartbeat thudded in her ears until…

The ball shot off at an angle before slamming straight into Brooke Bitmap's shoe and heading

back across the field to the other team's goalposts!

"That Brooke Bitmap," Millie said, seething. "She's slipped a magnet into the ball. Look, her shoes have metal plates on them!"

"Quasar College never did know how to play fair!" snorted Halinka.

"Pretty clever idea though," Millie said.

The two friends nodded in agreement.

The referee's whistle interrupted them.

"Pearl Peppersmith and Brooke Bitmap, please leave the field. There is no cheating permitted," the ref said, holding up a red card.

Pearl made her way over to her friends on the sidelines, where Halinka had already been disqualified for using a telescopic grabber arm to poke other players in the ribs. They watched as Miss Bunsen argued with the referee as to

whether this was cheating or simply an ana-
tomical design improvement.

The referee's whistle blew again. And again.
Other girls were disqualified for hiding jet
packs under their shirts and greasing their
opponents' shoes, and Sophie Syntax was sent
off for creating a force field across the goalposts
that made scoring impossible.

"Well," Pearl said, "what do you expect when
you get several science and engineering schools
together at a sports competition? There will be
improvisation and inventive ways of bending
the rules!"

"Look up there," Millie said, squinting her
eyes at the sun. "Is that a...squirrel?"

"Not just one," Halinka said, putting her
head in her hands. "I guess Miss Bunsen's will
use any means necessary to win a game, even a
squirrel attack!"

The referee's whistle was now in danger of breaking from over-use. "NO SQUIRRELS ON THE FIELD!"

The annual Girls of Science Games Day had been held at the end of the school year for as long as anyone could remember. Miss Bunsen herself was rumored to have taken part in the games once, although nobody in living memory could prove it.

Pearl nestled herself between her friends on the grass and sighed.

"What's up?" asked Millie. "Are you okay?"

"Kind of. Last night, my parents told me that they're working all summer and can't have anyone watch me during the day. I have to go and stay at my aunt's house on the other side of the river, and I won't be able to spend the summer holidays with you two."

"That's terrible!" Millie gasped. "I can't go six weeks without you."

"I've got a bit of news myself," Halinka added, looking uncharacteristically serious. "My parents are sending me to Velocity College summer school."

"Summer school's not bad," said Millie wistfully. "Maybe you can take advanced math!"

"But if it's any good, they said they might take me out of Miss Bunsen's altogether and send me to Velocity College permanently!"

"But why?!" both Millie and Pearl gasped together.

"They said Miss Bunsen's doesn't have the

money or facilities to give me the best opportunities in life. They sounded serious."

"That's ridiculous!" Pearl replied.

"I know, but it's also kind of true," said Halinka glumly. She gestured toward the other schools at the games. "Look around. Atom runs a summer exchange program with a top technical college in China, Quasar College spends summer at the Young Women's Institute  for Rocket Science, and Velocity has the option to board all summer with weekly guest speakers including the country's top scientists, engineers, and designers."

"So if you were to go to Velocity, we wouldn't

even see you during breaks?" squeaked Millie.

Halinka shook her head.

"Miss Bunsen's school has no plans for the
summer holidays, nothing
apart from squirrel control
and patching up a leaky, old
roof."

Pearl gazed at her feisty
friend, and a funny, anxious
feeling crept into her tummy. Did Halinka
secretly want to go to Velocity? Maybe she had
realized that Miss Bunsen's school wasn't up to
scratch.

The three friends looked out over the sunny
sports field, the warm summer heat not even
able to lift their mood. They realized that, this
summer, they would be apart for the first time
ever—and maybe even for good.

Chapter 2

A crackling speaker made them jump, and they turned to watch a large screen that was positioned over the field. Up onstage, the commentator spoke with a voice that sounded like he was holding his nose.

"Would everybody please give a warm welcome to our special guest: famed astronaut Nova Celeste!"

"Is that really her?" Millie said, her voice shaking.

"Yes, yes it is," replied Pearl as the three

friends moved closer to the field to get a better view.

The commentator continued in his nasally voice. "I'm sure I don't have to tell any of you clever young scientists much about our special guest. You probably already know all about her, but in case you have been living under a moon rock, allow me to remind you."

Nova blushed a little and shook her head modestly, grasping tightly onto the space helmet tucked under her arm.

"Nova is the chief commander at Star Village Space Center and has trained the best astronauts that this country has ever seen. She has made seventeen flights into space, twelve of which were complete orbits around the Earth, and at one time was the youngest person ever to leave the Earth's atmosphere. Along with designing the fastest, lightest, and most

environmentally friendly superplane, she is a pioneer of using eco-friendly engineering materials, a topic she fights passionately for with her—"

"Let me interrupt you there," Nova said sweetly, pushing down the commentator's microphone. "This is about the girls, not me!"

She stepped forward, her voice so strong and clear that she didn't need the microphone to be heard. "Young women of science, I am here to give you a challenge."

The crowd began to whisper, and a wave of excitement washed over the stadium.

"Now, I know you ladies have a busy schedule with foreign exchanges and summer camps and all kinds of other summer business going on, but I understand that you all have a week free in July, so here's the thing..."

Pearl, Millie, and Halinka glanced at one

another, realizing this was sounding like a way out of their pickle.

"I need a craft—a craft that can fly over Lake Cosmos without anybody getting wet. The machine can hold only one person, and extra points will be awarded for good use of materials, so think environmentally friendly. The flight that makes it from one side of the lake to the other in the shortest amount of time will be the winner. It's that simple. The prize?"

Everyone listened intently.

"I'm opening up the doors of Star Village Space Center for one team and one team only. This is a chance to get access to the most up-to-date and high-tech space hardware and equipment known on Earth and be taught by some of the most experienced astronauts ever to fly into space. You'll learn how to use critical thinking to solve problems that you would face in a real-life space mission, and you will explore space in simulated flights and experience weightlessness in our specially designed simulator. And at the end of the week, for the grand finale, you'll fly into orbit in our shuttle—with me as your captain."

The entire stadium fell silent, stunned at the news of the contest and the reward, before erupting into cheers and screams of excitement.

"WAIT!" Nova continued, and everyone quieted down again. "This isn't any ordinary prize for any ordinary young scientist. I'm looking for skill. I'm looking for design brilliance. And"—Nova slowly moved her outstretched finger around the stadium, a determined expression on her face—"I'm looking for something different."

Then she turned and left the stage, followed by a flurry of head teachers. Pearl thought she saw Miss Bunsen running to keep up.

She swung around to her friends so fast she nearly fell over.

"THIS IS IT!!! We *have* to win this. Halinka, if

your parents find out you are going to study at Star Village Space Center, they're going to forget ALL about Velocity College. And I won't have to spend the entire summer at my aunt's, and we can all be together for at least a week."

Millie was standing stock-still, her face turned to where Nova Celeste was standing only moments earlier. "It was really her! I have a full-size cardboard cutout of her in my room. I can't believe we were nearly breathing the same air!"

"Oh, Millie," Halinka said, rolling her eyes, "you're such a fangirl."

Millie pushed her glasses back up her nose, looking slightly embarrassed.

"You're right," she said, quickly pulling out her notebook and three carrot-and-granola bars from her bag. She grinned. "Let's get a head start on this. I'm not about to lose you—or a chance at working with Nova Celeste! Did you know that Nova eats one of these every morning after her workout?" she said, offering the tasty bars to her friends.

"I'm not sure that even a hundred of these carrot-and-granola bars will help us win this." Halinka sighed, looking around at the other more high-tech schools that would be entering the competition too.

"You don't sound like you even care," Pearl said, becoming more convinced her friend had given up on Miss Bunsen's School for Brilliant Girls altogether.

"Of course I care!" Halinka seemed slightly offended. "Now pass me that sketchbook."

Soon the gloomy atmosphere had cleared, and the girls giggled and crowded over Millie's notebook, muttering and drawing. Pearl sketched several models of flying machines, each more elaborate than the last. Millie dove into calculations for flight paths, and Halinka drew different kinds of engines they could use.

And as the shadows over the stadium grew longer and the air grew cooler, Pearl watched as the moon rose up in the pale blue sky.

"We must win this," she whispered to herself. "We must win this."

Chapter 3

The next morning, just as the sun was rising, already burning hot, and the squirrels of Miss Bunsen's were getting ready for another day of mischief, Pearl and her two friends slowly shuffled themselves up the hill.

"I'm so tired." Halinka yawned. "I was up really late putting the finishing touches on my beloved Turbo Trike. I've totally modified it. Next time you see it, you'll scream!"

"And I drank the last of the Cherryade I've been using to fuel my new fizzy fun Fruitboard."

Millie sighed. "I could really use some now. It's so warm already!"

"I wish that's why *I* was up late. Miss Bunsen had me look after Brains last night, and his bottom exploded all over my scooter." Pearl gestured to the guilty looking ball of fluff and metal poking out from her backpack.

"Well, at least we have a stack of ideas to get working on in the new engineering suite. It's nice to put that prize money from Professor Petrinsky to work!" Millie said with glee, holding up the bulging notebook they had filled with drawings, diagrams, graphs, and equations the evening before.

"You call *that* an engineering suite?" came a shrill voice from behind them.

"More like an engineering cupboard of junk" came a second voice.

Pearl, Millie, and Halinka all took deep breaths before turning around to face Megan and Heather.

"Ladies," Pearl said, trying her best to be civil and friendly, "how are we this morning?"

"Sounds like we're doing better than you three snorers. Why don't you just go back to bed? We've already got this

competition in the bag." Megan looked down and stroked the pearly white scooter by her side, its smooth lines glimmering in the sunshine.

"Yeah," Heather continued, "you weren't the only ones up late online shopping, er, I mean, designing."

"What on earth even is that?" Halinka sniffed. She tried to look indifferent but was unable to take her eyes off the shimmering, white scooter and the glittery residue that seemed to be trailing behind it. The Atom Academy scooters had always been nice and neat, but something seemed different about this one.

"This," Megan said snootily, "is the result of many hours of chemical experiments. We came up with exactly the correct formula to achieve—drum roll, please—Freezacon. We built this scooter out of it last night, and we're going to build our flying craft out of it today."

"Freezacon? Never heard of it," Halinka said.

"Well, duh! You wouldn't have done. We invented it last night."

"You two invented something?" Halinka snorted.

"So what's with all the white, flaky stuff?" Pearl asked, looking at the mess on the ground.

"I've got a cream for that." Millie giggled. Halinka and Pearl looked at her, shocked but amused. Millie usually was so scared of Heather and Megan that she couldn't speak, let alone joke.

Heather rolled her eyes. "Oh. My. Grommets. And you actually think you have a chance of winning? Why it's a built-in snow machine! Nova Celeste said she wanted 'something different,' remember? So our flying machine will create its very own snow."

The Bunseners exchanged glances and looked back at the scooter.

"If that's the case, shouldn't there be some sort of fan—" began Millie meekly.

Megan interrupted her. "Come on, Heather. Let's leave these boiled-cabbage-brained Bunseners to it."

Heather trotted after her friend, coughing and spluttering as she walked into a face full of scooter residue.

"And you won't have your little friend to help you this time, ha!" she managed to shout.

"What do you mean?" Pearl called after Heather. But they were gone, with nothing but a trail of white mess to show they had been there at all.

"Oh, they talk such nonsense!" Millie huffed, watching the concern on Pearl's face grow. "Come on. Let's do what Nova would do—get to work!"

Pearl smiled at her kind friend and pushed open the rusty green gates of Miss Bunsen's school. "Looks like we're the first ones here this morning."

"Not quite" came a croaky, little voice from behind the ivy of the gatehouse.

The girls stopped in their tracks, looking about to see where the voice was coming from.

"Oh, Miss Crankitt," Pearl said shakily as the old lady began to emerge from the greenery that covered the old gatehouse. "It's you!"

"I thought the squirrels had learned to talk!" Halinka said, clutching her chest.

Miss Crankitt had been living in the gatehouse at Miss Bunsen's since before the squirrels had arrived—some said maybe even before Miss Bunsen herself had taken over. Nobody quite knew why she was there, but she was encouraged to stay and watch over the school.

Rumors flew about Miss Crankitt. Second years whispered she could tell the future, third years thought she was a ghost, and Mr. Bell, the caretaker, believed that Miss Bunsen's School for Brilliant Girls might fall if Miss Crankitt left.

Miss Crankitt leaned toward the girls and lifted a bony hand up to the sky. As she adjusted her headpiece, she said:

"Never say it's
   only me.
Never think it's
   only you.
Like two bright
   sides of the moon,
It can never ever
   snow in June."

The three girls stood in silence for a second.

"What does that mean?" Millie squeaked quietly.

"I think we should probably get out of here," Halinka suggested, her voice uncharacteristically shaky.

"Okay, great! Thanks, Miss Crankitt," Pearl said politely, grabbing her friends by the arms and ushering them away slowly from the mysterious old lady. "We've got to be going to class now. We've got a flying machine to build!"

Miss Crankitt disappeared behind the foliage again as more and more Bunseners arrived for school.

"What do you think she meant?" Millie asked as they swooped up the steep school steps. "Did any of that make sense? Two bright sides of the moon?"

"She's probably been drinking out of the rain

gauge again," Halinka said, trying to lighten the mood, which had turned a little spooky.

"I don't know," Pearl said thoughtfully. "Miss Crankitt doesn't often talk to students, and she does have a kind of sixth sense."

"Don't be ridiculous, Pearl," Halinka snapped. "We're scientists. We don't believe in airy-fairy nonsense. We rely on the facts, on figures and numbers, and, and…"

"Equilateral triangles," Millie offered helpfully.

The look on Halinka's face showed that wasn't exactly what she had been searching for.

Pearl followed her two friends into school, feeling slightly unnerved by Miss

Crankitt's rare appearance. But stewing on a spooky old lady's riddle wouldn't help build a flying machine, so Pearl pushed the words to the back of her mind.

Chapter 4

"Our first time using the engineering suite, and it's for something *so exciting*!" Millie gushed as she threw her bag on the workbench. Her papers flew across the surface, and she sighed happily. "There's so much space!"

She flicked on two computer monitors and began frantically typing numbers and letters into the keyboard.

"I just love these Ametz 24 computers," Millie said, pushing her glasses up her nose and watching the screen display in front of her. "Did you know Nova Celeste has the latest Ametz 25 at her space camp?"

"You really are a fangirl!" Halinka laughed. "So, let's get building! Where do we start?"

"Okay, so according to this flight simulation software, there are a few options for the best design from our sketches," Millie said, showing Pearl and Halinka the 3-D images on the computer screen. "Personally, I like this one that Halinka designed. It's powered by battery, it's

manageable, it's safe, and we can definitely get it done."

"What about the one that Pearl designed, here?" Halinka said, pointing to the screen with a chewed piece of straw.

"Well, it's genius, but it's not something I've seen before—it might not work."

"But if it did, it would be spectacular," Halinka argued.

"I don't mind if we want to build Halinka's," Pearl said, not wanting to upset anyone.

"I like Pearl's the best. It's got class, and it's totally creative." Halinka held up the detailed drawing for them to study.

Pearl felt relieved that her friend thought she was a good scientist after all and not just a silly

Billy for believing Miss Crankitt's gibberish.

"Well, let's try it out," Millie said, pressing Print and waiting for the blueprint to roll out of the printer. Halinka grabbed the large paper printout and laid it out on the table, poring over the beautiful aerodynamic shapes that Pearl had designed.

"We've got all the material here we need," Pearl said, feeling a wave of confidence wash over her as she watched her two friends study her design.

"We can use the recycled drink can's metal for the body of the craft, as it's so lightweight, and the fabric that was upcycled from the lost-and-found box can make up the wings."

Before Pearl could even finish her sentence, there was a pile of materials on the workbench. Halinka and Millie began hammering and cutting out metal, filling the lab with clattering sounds. The smell of soldering irons from the group on the bench beside them wafted into the air, the engineering suite full of Bunseners busily working away on their flying contraptions. As the day wore on, more and more wonderful inventions began to materialize, and soon the three friends were standing in front of their very own wonderful flying machine.

There was a main body of the craft, with a

seat made from recycled rubber bands and just enough room for one girl to squeeze in. A compression pump was neatly tucked away underneath the seat, and two foot pedals provided the pressure needed to push the air up to the wings. The wings swept beautifully along the side of the craft and would flap silently and gracefully, powered by a specially designed solar motor. The whole machine could be steered using one single stick made from the shiniest polished metal. A tiny diesel engine would spark up for takeoff, giving the craft just enough power to get into the air before shutting down and letting it rely on natural power.

"If my flight trajectory calculations are correct, we should need only a small amount of diesel to give us a

push off, and then the wings and velocity, plus the wind direction, should be enough to make it across Lake Cosmos," said Pearl. "We don't need fuel for the entire flight because we used such lightweight materials—we can make dual use of the foot pumps to flap the wings. And it's going to be windy tomorrow afternoon, so we can harness the power of nature to really make our machine fly!"

"But what about what Nova Celeste said about having something different, like Heather and Megan's snow machine?" Millie asked, nervously looking around at all the other Bunseners and their contraptions. "I can't see anything in here that's really that different."

"But, Millie," Pearl said, feeling a little hurt that her friend wasn't overly impressed with her design, "we *are* different. We're Bunsen girls. We'll always stand out—sometimes without meaning to. We don't need a gimmick, like a snow machine, and I'm not sure that even was a snow machine on that scooter anyway."

"You're not still going on about what Miss Crankitt said, are you?" Halinka said, scoffing as she popped a piece of carrot granola bar from Millie's bag into her mouth.

"Well, no," Pearl replied, feeling a little flushed with embarrassment and wondering if her friends' opinions of her could get any worse. "I was actually thinking about why the snow wasn't melting. It was so hot this morning, and the melting point of water is 32°Fahrenheit/0°Celsius. So how did all that 'snow' just sit on the street?"

Halinka stopped chewing, and Millie pushed

her glasses up her nose.

"And I don't want to be mean, but..." Pearl hesitated.

Halinka finished Pearl's sentence. "How could two unbelievably lazy, mean girls invent anything?"

"Yes, that's about the measure of it," Pearl continued. "I'm sorry to bring up Miss Crankitt, but she's right. It cannot snow in June when it's this warm. Just like there can't be two bright sides of the moon. It's a scientific impossibility."

"So if it isn't snow coming off the scooter, what is it?" Millie asked.

"Exactly."

"Well, they copied our designs once. Maybe they copied this. Let me check this out a second," Millie said, pulling out her *A–Z of Amazing Compounds, Elements, and Seriously Sassy Substances*. "This is the only copy left in

print. It has every chemical substance dating back all the way to the eighteenth century! Esters, Ethers, Fermium, Ferrum…Freezacon! It's in here!" Millie shrieked.

"What does it say?" Halinka and Pearl huddled around Millie as she read out loud:

"'Freezacon is a lightweight material invented in 1955 and used in the engineering and manufacture of spaceships and rockets and other high-orbit-flying crafts. It was banned only a year later, after it was found that, when exposed to direct sunlight, a white, powdery residue flaked off, making any craft built from Freezacon very weak and prone to disintegrating midflight!'"

Halinka squinted up at the blazing sun in the sky above them.

"Like the direct sunshine we have today!" she said.

"But that's not all," Millie said gravely. "If the Freezacon comes into contact with water, it…"

"It what?" Pearl asked.

"It explodes! We need to warn Heather and Megan!" Millie shrieked, stuffing the sketchbook of designs into her bag.

"But everyone else is taking their flying machines out into the yard for test flights!" Halinka harrumphed.

"Millie's right," said Pearl. "We can leave our machine in the engineering lab for now and test it later. It's more important that we warn Heather and Megan that they could get hurt. Time to take a trip up the hill to Atom!"

Chapter 5

It was fairly easy to sneak out of Miss Bunsen's School without anybody noticing, as everyone was so busy building their flying machines. Apart from having to bat off a few squirrels, Pearl, Millie, and Halinka were soon on their way up the hill toward Atom Academy.

"The gates are locked." Halinka sighed, rattling the shiny, geometric gates. "And we know better than to try to break in again."

"But we need to speak to Megan and Heather ASAP," Pearl said, ringing the buzzer.

A security camera mounted up high on the gate swung around and pointed at the three girls before a robotic voice came through the intercom.

"Yes, visitor. Please state your intention."

"Um, we need to speak to Megan McNebulus and Heather Etherson. It's a matter of urgency."

The camera made a noise as if it were zooming in closer to the girls. "Face recognition activated. You are banned. You are banned. Security mode activated!"

"But Megan and Heather are in danger!" Pearl continued.

"SECURITY MODE ACTIVATED. THREE, TWO, ONE…"

When she rang the buzzer again, she shot backward and landed on her bottom. "It electrocuted me!" she said with a shiver.

"Are you okay?" Millie asked, gingerly putting

her arm around her friend.

"I'm fine. It was very low voltage. Just enough to get rid of me."

Pearl stood up and dusted herself off when suddenly the girls' attention was drawn to a funny noise coming from the bottom of the hill.

"Is that…?" Millie began.

"The fire alarm!" Halinka shrieked.

The three girls raced back down the hill where, sure enough, in between all the flying machines in the yard, the whole school was lined up. Even the squirrels sat neatly outside along the street. There was a fire engine hosing down a little hole in the roof, and Miss Bunsen was talking to one of the firefighters.

He pointed to the friends running down the hill, and Miss Bunsen turned, a relieved smile spreading across her face.

"What happened, Miss Bunsen?" asked

Halinka, running up to her.

"Oh, girls!" she cried. "We evacuated the school. Everyone is safe, but we panicked when we couldn't find you. These three are the last to be accounted for, sir," she said, nodding to the firefighter.

"Oh. Miss Bunsen, we're so sorry to have worried you," Pearl said. "We had tried to visit Atom—"

"Yes, yes, we'll have to sort that out later," Miss Bunsen said, waving them away. "Right now, we have a disaster on our hands. It's the engineering suite!"

"What about the engineering suite?" Pearl asked, horrified.

The firefighter responded. "Rodents seem to have gnawed through the wiring and caused a small fire."

"Rodents?" asked Pearl.

"Those *squirrels*!" growled Halinka. "They've got to go, Miss Bunsen!"

"Is it ruined?" Millie asked, her hands covering her ears as though she didn't want to hear the answer.

"No, it should be fine with a bit of a clean,

but the firefighters have closed it off as a precaution. We don't know if our furry friends got to any other wires, so it's too dangerous to turn anything on."

"But surely we can get in there," Pearl said, pleading. "Our invention is inside!"

The firefighter shook his head. "I'm afraid it's

out of the question until we have the chance to inspect the building. Our wiring expert will be in once the break begins, and you're all safely on your holidays."

The girls gasped.

"Miss Bunsen, how can we enter the competition without our flying craft?" asked Pearl.

"I'm quite sure you three have the ingenuity to think of something. I don't raise my Bunseners to let a small fire make them give up!" And then, after giving them a theatrical wink, she swept off, counting and recounting her Bunseners again and again just to be completely sure they had all escaped the building.

"I hate those squirrels," said Halinka. "There goes our chance of winning the competition."

"And of us being together this summer," Millie sobbed.

"And of Halinka staying at Miss Bunsen's!"

cried Pearl. She thought for a second before spinning around to face her friends.

"Okay," she said firmly. "Miss Bunsen is right. We can't give up. We had *one* problem."

"Trying to warn Heather and Megan about their dangerous material?" Millie asked.

"Yes," Pearl replied, and nodded toward the thin plume of smoke emerging from the hole in the roof. "And now we have two."

"I can think of a few dozen other problems," Halinka said, glaring angrily at the line of guilty-looking squirrels.

"You know what? We can sort both of them, but we'll have to be quick and we'll have to improvise…a lot!" Pearl smiled.

"Well, that's what we're good at!" Halinka winked at Millie.

"So what's the plan?!" Millie asked eagerly

Pearl crouched down on the sidewalk, grabbed a stone, and began to scribble away, her two friends hovering above her eager to see what they were challenged to do.

"Millie, you've still got a Grrl Bot in your locker, right?"

"Sure do."

"Okay, so let's program her to fly to Atom and deliver a message to Heather and Megan. We can then have the Grrl Bot returned to us with a message from Heather and Megan, so we're sure they know of the danger."

"Boom! One problem down, one to go," said Halinka.

"Next, we need to build our flying craft without the engineering suite, which is going to be the tricky part." Pearl put her finger to her forehead.

"That seems like an understatement," said Halinka.

"I've still got this!" Millie pulled out Pearl's original drawing from her sketchbook.

"Brilliant!" Pearl gushed, grabbing the precious diagram from Millie.

"Halinka, I need you to scour the school and the bins for anything we can use to build this thing again. It won't be perfect, but at least we'll still have a chance! Millie, can you help me scale up this drawing, so we know how much stuff we'll need?"

"Well, th-th-the thing is," Millie stuttered, "this design was brilliant when we had the engineering suite and the Ametz 24 computers to figure out the calculations for the flight trajectory, but trying to build this machine and make it fly by just working out the numbers in our heads is risky. We could end up getting very wet."

Millie flicked through the sketchbook of designs. "We could use Halinka's design instead," she suggested, pointing to the much simpler drawing. "We could definitely get this built and across the lake, no problem."

Pearl wondered if Millie thought Halinka was a better engineer than Pearl. After all, she hadn't been so keen on using Pearl's design in the first place.

Halinka's face flushed with excitement before suddenly becoming more serious.

"No," she said, looking at Pearl. "Pearl is the best designer among us. I may be a whiz at mechanics and making stuff, but Pearl is our girl when it comes to creativity, and that is what Nova Celeste is looking for. Sure, my design will get us safely and easily across the lake, but that's not the Bunsen spirit. We're going to build Pearl's craft! Even if it ends up at the bottom of Lake Cosmos as a glorified fish house, at least we tried."

There was a moment of silence while the girls let the enormity of their task sink in.

"Let's do this," Pearl said, leaning in to hug Halinka. Maybe she had been worried about losing her friend for nothing.

"No time for hugs!" Halinka shouted, ducking out of the way. "We've got a flying machine to build. And unless someone stops me, I've got some squirrels that I need to visit!"

The friends laughed as Halinka pantomimed her trademark squirrel battle dance.

"We'll need to decide what to make it out of," said Millie, looking about the yard doubtfully.

"I'll find you something to build with, Millie.

I promise," said Halinka.

"Thanks, Halinka," said Millie.

As the rest of the school filed back inside, the friends began scouring the school for parts. They had some building to do.

Chapter 6

Halinka plonked a large and slightly soggy cardboard box down onto the playground floor.

"That's all I could find," she said as she watched Millie and Pearl pick through the junk. They'd found everything from empty tomato cans in the kitchen rubbish to some twisty, old hoses Mr. Bell, the caretaker, had let them use.

Pearl held up two electric whisks, examining them closely before turning to Millie. "Do you think we can convert these to run on battery power?"

"We could, but batteries big enough to keep those spinning for the whole flight across Lake Cosmos would be very heavy," Millie said, trying to resist the urge to push her glasses up her nose.

"Hmmm, anyone got any chalk?" Pearl asked.

Halinka reached behind her ear and flicked a stick of blue chalk over to her friend. Pearl started scribbling on the ground.

"So, if we cut out the seat of this shopping trolley and attach it to these two sewing machines, we've got a start to the body of the craft."

Halinka and Millie watched with their heads cocked as they listened closely

to their clever friend.

"These pedals will turn the handle of the sewing machines, pushing the needles up and down, trapping compressed air into these tomato cans underneath. The compressed air will then shoot through these old pieces of hose pipe and power the whisks, onto which Millie can weld two propellers, which, once in flight, should be enough to push the craft across Lake Cosmos."

"What propellers?" Millie asked, looking befuddled.

"Four serving spoons bolted together like this!" Pearl held up her contraption, smiling.

"But how are we going to get the wings to flap, now that we don't have access to all the solar power motors that were in the engineering suite?" Halinka asked. "And what are they going to be made from?"

Pearl pulled a huge tattered umbrella out from underneath one of the boxes.

"Ta-da!" She smiled, twirling it about and looking very pleased with herself.

Millie and Halinka both stood studying the chalk drawing.

"Well," Halinka said, "if you're sure it'll work, then let's get building."

"It has to work. We can't be split up. We *must* win this competition," Pearl said.

They looked determinedly at each other. They would *not* split up for good.

Chapter 7

"Mmm, this spinach-and-raspberry smoothie is gooood!" Pearl said to Millie, who had arrived at the school gates on her Smoothie-Making Penny-Farthing.

"Here," Millie said to Halinka, passing her a bottle of green gloop. "Try this walnut-and-kiwi smoothie. It'll set you right up for a day of flying!"

"No thanks!" Halinka said, turning up her nose. "I don't want to attract any squirrels, so it's best to avoid anything with nuts!"

"Suit yourself." Millie shrugged before guzzling down the gloop herself.

A loud swooshing noise from above caused the three friends to look up.

"It's the Grrl Bot! Megan and Heather must have sent a reply!" Pearl said in a relieved tone.

Halinka reached up and retrieved the Grrl Bot from the tree where it had landed using her telescopic grabber arm, and the three girls flicked the switch to watch the monitor on the Grrl Bot's tummy.

A grainy black-and-white image appeared, but it was clearly Heather and Megan.

"Turn it up, Halinka," said Pearl as they struggled to hear the muffled message.

"Nice try, Bunsen burnouts! We know your

game. You're trying to get us to
step down from the competition,
so you have a better chance
of winning. Well, bad luck!
See you at Lake Cosmos this
afternoon!"

"Are they really that
stupid?" Halinka said, her
mouth hanging open.

"They think we're trying to trick them?"
Millie said. "But we're trying to save them!"

"I guess, because they're so mean, they
assume everyone else is too," Pearl said, wondering what to do now.

"Look," Halinka said, "we tried our best. We
can just tell the organizers this afternoon when
we get there. They won't let Atom take part if
students are in danger."

"At least we tried," said Millie. "That's

probably more than they would do."

"Now for the most important part: the test flight!" Pearl said, leading her two friends onto the playground, where they had left the flying machine overnight.

"No sign of any squirrel damage," Halinka said, inspecting the machine. "For once."

Millie made a few final adjustments before helping Pearl up onto the seat and making sure the wings were positioned correctly.

"Ready for takeoff?" Millie said, licking her finger and holding it up to the sky to test the wind direction.

"I think so," Pearl replied, shakily pulling her goggles down over her eyes and nervously looking out at the long stretch of playground in front of her.

Pearl held her finger down on the small silver button on the top of the left lever and waited for the engine to spark up.

"It's not doing anything!" Halinka said, panicking.

"Let me just adjust the wiring," Millie said, poking her screwdriver into the control panel.

Suddenly, instead of steadily coursing along the runway and gliding into the air smoothly, the machine shot straight up! It flipped over, leaving Pearl hanging upside down, like a fruit bat.

"What's it doing?" Pearl shrieked.

"Use the levers!" Millie shouted from far below. "Pull the left one back and push the right one forward a little!"

Pearl maneuvered the levers, and the flying machine flipped back up the right way.

"Now flap your wings!" shouted Halinka.

Pearl pulled the two levers at her side, and gradually, her umbrella wings began to flap back and forth.

"It works. I'm flying!" Pearl cried as she glided about above the rickety rooftops of Miss Bunsen's school.

"Go, Pearl!" Halinka shrieked, jumping up and down and clapping wildly.

"I'm feeling a bit emotional," Millie said, wiping a little tear away from her eye. "It looks like we have a chance of all staying together after all." She and Halinka hugged each other tightly, not noticing that Pearl and the machine had started to lose altitude in rapid bursts.

"COMING THROOOOOUUUGH!" Pearl hollered as the machine suddenly dove toward the ground before swooping back up just in time.

"What's it doing now?" Pearl cried. "I can't control it!"

"Watch out, Mr. Bell!" Millie cried as the old caretaker jumped out of the way just before

Pearl flew at speed up the school steps and in through the school's front doors.

Pearl corkscrewed her way along the main corridor before bursting though the main hall doors, where Bunseners were gathering for morning assembly. She flew in out-of-control circles above their heads.

"Coming down!" Pearl shouted, covering her eyes. When she reopened them, she had somehow exited the school and had Brains clinging to her back.

Slowly, the machine descended back onto the playground, where Millie and Halinka were running around beneath her, trying to figure out a way to cushion her landing if she kept falling.

"It started flying smoothly again! I don't get it," Pearl said, pushing her goggles back onto her forehead.

"It suddenly seems to be working okay."

Millie looked confused.

"It's a miracle recovery!" Halinka said.

"The flying machine was totally out of control! It was only when I somehow acquired Brains on board that the whole thing began to fly a little better, but it's still not perfect!"

"Oh, good boy, Brains!" Millie said, lifting the ball of fur and scrap metal down from the flying machine and giving him a tight squeeze.

"Don't squeeze him too t... Oh. Too late," Pearl said, looking at the trickle of wee running down Millie's shirt.

"Look!" Halinka said, suddenly pointing to Brains's back. "What's this?"

"It looks like some sort of turbocharger," Millie said. The three friends looked more closely at the small pack

on the cat's back, which had a long metal pipe bending out from it.

"That's it!" Millie shrieked excitedly. "It needs more power on takeoff and landing to set the craft on a straight trajectory. If there's not enough power, the flying machine won't gain enough velocity and will just lose control."

"So we need to attach the turbocharger to the engine?" Halinka asked.

"Ideally, yes," Millie said. "Problem is this charger is done—it's too damaged and old now to reuse, and I don't have the time or the equipment to build a new one before the competition."

"I guess that's it then. We're doomed to get wet," Pearl said, looking at the flying machine with a tear in her eye.

"All that hard work for nothing." Millie whimpered.

"Look," Pearl said. "Everyone is starting to move their machines down to the lake."

"Come on. You need to get this machine down to Lake Cosmos and at least give it a go," said Halinka. "I'll meet you there." She pulled her backpack onto her shoulder and strode off.

Pearl watched her friend disappear out of the gate and wondered again why she didn't even seem slightly upset. Maybe her worries that Halinka didn't care because she really didn't want to stay at Miss Bunsen's that badly anymore were right after all. Did she want to make some new friends at Velocity College? Maybe Pearl wasn't a clever enough friend anymore for Halinka and Millie—after all, now her flying machine didn't even work.

Millie started trying to lug their machine across the grounds, but Pearl stood still for a moment. If they didn't win this competition, they'd be split up—but maybe that was what Millie and Halinka wanted.

Chapter 8

With a warm breeze blowing, the girls of Miss Bunsen's School for Brilliant Girls began to wheel, push, and carry their amazing and not-so-amazing flying machines down to Lake Cosmos to compete for the grand prize.

"Oh, wow!" Millie looked around at the rows of incredible flying machines all lined up along the bank of Lake Cosmos from all the science schools in the area.

Sienna and Sophie from Miss Bunsen's were busy polishing the nose cone of their

sprout-fueled rocket.

"Oh, Sienna," Millie said, "this invention is an awesome way to use up all those sprouts that no one ever eats!"

Sienna laughed. "I guess they're good for something!"

"Just not lunch," Sophie added. "We've got enough gas built up in this little chamber to get us across the lake, I hope!" She patted the three tiny cylinders on the side of the rocket.

"We're really lucky that we were testing

82

it out on the playground when the fire in the engineering suite broke out," Sienna said. "I'm so sorry you guys had your design trapped in there."

"Thanks, Sienna," Pearl said. "We tried to build something else, but who knows if it'll make it across?"

Just then, Millie let out a loud shriek.

"Look!" she gasped. "There's Nova Celeste!"

The Bunsen girls watched in awe as Nova drove up in her electric car, but their view was

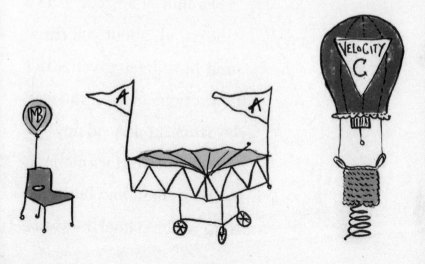

soon blocked by a tall figure.

"SCHOOL?" demanded a woman. She was clutching a clipboard so tightly her knuckles were white.

"Erm, Miss Bunsen's," Pearl replied, pointing at the badge on her blouse.

"No need to be snippy, Pearl Peppersmith," the woman sniffed. "I've heard all about you three and have been given strict instructions to keep you well away from Atom Academy."

Pearl wondered for a moment why the woman had bothered asking which school they were

84

from if she already knew who they were but concluded that the snooty lady probably just liked shouting "SCHOOL?" at children.

"But, miss," Millie chirped, "we absolutely must speak with you about the flying machine being entered by Megan and Heather. It's…"

"ENOUGH!" the clipboard lady snapped. "You are not to mention anything about Atom. They have made it quite clear that you are to be kept well away from them, as your meddling and troublemaking is causing a terrible nuisance. Now keep quiet and stay out of trouble."

A familiar nasal voice began to echo around the competition grounds. "The contest is about to begin. Atom Academy, please take your places at the side of the lake."

"Oh no! Atom is going first, and it looks like Megan and Heather are front of the queue!" Millie gasped. "We have to warn them!"

Millie burst out of the line she was in and ran toward Heather and Megan and their shiny, white flying machine, but before she could get to them, an arm reached out and pulled her back. It was the snooty clipboard lady.

"I warned you once! Now you are going to have to stay with me," she snarled through yellow teeth. She looked at the yellow stain on Millie's blouse. "Is that cat wee I smell?"

"Millie, you must make them listen about the Freezacon! You take care of that, and I'll deal with the flight," Pearl called after her friend.

"I'll make sure they listen!" Millie called back as she was dragged away.

"Millie's been caught!" Pearl said, panicking. "How am I going to get the machine started without her help?!" Brains was the only one listening to her. "And where is Halinka?"

Brains looked up at Pearl with his one good

eye before coughing up a fur ball, some nuts and bolts, and a piece of copper wire of surprising length.

The nasally voice continued. "Will Megan and Heather please prepare for takeoff?"

"This could be really bad. Why haven't they been stopped?" Pearl said with genuine concern. She watched as Megan climbed into the swanky, glittery, streamlined, white machine with a row of blue lights along each wing.

Heather did the preflight checks before standing back, looking smug.

The sleek machine began to roll along the grass runway before effortlessly soaring up into the air.

Pearl watched closely, desperately hoping that Atom's machine made it across the lake. Heather and Megan may have been mean girls, but she would never want them to get hurt.

Suddenly, Brains began to fidget.

"What's the matter, you silly old cat?" Pearl said before realizing that Brains was trying to point with a grubby paw toward the surface of the lake.

"What is that?" Pearl whispered under her breath, pulling out a pair of tiny binoculars from her shirt pocket.

Floating on the surface of the water, hundreds of tiny flames of white light.

"That must be where the Freezacon is flaking off and coming into contact with the water in the lake!" she gasped.

Nervously, she and Brains watched as Atom's flying machine reached full height over the center of the lake.

"Look at them go!" the commentator blared.

The craft began to descend, and Pearl covered her eyes.

"Wow, what a flight!" The commentator cheered as Megan landed safely on the other side of the lake. "And only 22.6 seconds!"

Pearl uncovered her eyes and sighed in relief.

Megan pulled off her ice-blue, sparkly helmet and shook her long, blond hair before speaking.

"What do you expect from the best academy in the city? I've been working on this special material for some time now, and as you can see, it's just perfect for a flying machine. Why, I even had time to add this special snow machine for dramatic effect. I know Nova was looking for something different, and I'm sure she'll be impressed."

Pearl listened to the selfish speech and glanced over at Heather, who was stamping her feet and shaking her fist at the other side of the lake where her "friend" was taking all the credit.

"Thank goodness they're okay," Pearl said to Brains.

The competition continued, and many brilliant, and some not-so-brilliant, contraptions flew over the lake.

There were elaborate inventions that hovered a few feet above the lake's surface and took forever to cross. There was Sophie and Sienna's incredible rocket, which zoomed over the lake in a flash! One girl was even shot across the lake from a giant catapult wearing a flying squirrel suit, only to land on a giant bouncy castle on the other side.

Some made it, and

some schoolgirls ended up very wet, but no one had beaten Atom's time yet.

"Next up," came the nasally voice, "Pearl, Halinka, and Millie from Miss Bunsen's School for Brilliant Girls."

"I can't do this by myself," Pearl said nervously as she popped Brains into the craft's seat and began heaving it to the start of the runway. She hoped that Brains could indeed help start the machine and wondered why her friend wasn't there to help.

"I guess Halinka must have found something better to do," she said to Brains, trying to hold back her tears.

Pearl climbed on board, adjusted the wings, and buckled herself in, while, as expected, Brains was unable to offer much help.

Just then, there was a loud roaring sound and a musical horn.

"Halinka!" Pearl shouted in a mix of panic and delight.

Chapter 9

Halinka revved her Turbo Trike engine as she zoomed over toward the flying machine before screeching to a halt. She jumped off her Turbo Trike and ripped off the turbo before quickly attaching it to the small engine at the back of the craft.

"That ought to see my clever friend over Lake Cosmos," Halinka said, winking at Pearl.

"But your Turbo Trike," Pearl gasped. "It's ruined now!"

"Well, I guess some things are more important than Turbo Trikes—NOT MANY, but my friendship with you is one of them."

Halinka took Brains and handed Pearl a long piece of wire with a button on the end. "Press this to shut off the diesel engine and turbo when you're in flight. Then, when you reach the other side, press it again to spark it up to help you land with more control."

Pearl sighed happily and pulled her goggles down over her eyes. She flicked the switch, and the engine roared to life. Halinka then pressed a button on the turbo, and the flying machine shot off down the runway.

"You can do this, Pearl. Flap, flap, flap for lift!" Millie shouted. She was standing awkwardly; her hands were being held behind her back by the clipboard lady.

"I think I've got this!" Pearl cried, buoyed by her friends' faith in her. She cruised elegantly up into the air and over the edge of Lake Cosmos. Then she pressed the button on the wire that Halinka had given her and shut off the engine and turbo.

But just then, there was a great thud on the back of the machine, and it lurched uncontrollably from side to side. It was Brains. He'd taken a heroic jump and landed on the

back of the flying machine.

"Brains, no! I don't need you. Jump off!"

But it was too late. The flying machine spiraled out of control. As Brains scrambled, his front paws covered Pearl's goggles, making it impossible for her to see where she was going.

"Come on, Pearl. Hold on. Hold on just a few more meters before you reach the other side," Halinka whispered, keeping everything crossed. "BRAINS! What are you doing, you silly old cat? Move your paws!"

But Pearl's flying machine spiraled down and down toward the lake.

"Oh, Brains," she said as the wind rushed past her ears, frantically trying to control the craft despite not being able to see a thing. "I think we might be about to get very wet!"

And sure enough, with a great splash, the flying machine landed just short of the edge of Lake Cosmos.

"Whoa!" the commentator cried, running over with his microphone, knee deep in water. "That was quite a landing! Can you tell me a little about your machine?"

"Yes," Pearl said, a little out of breath. "We originally had a better machine, but—"

"All righty!" the commentator interrupted.

"This isn't the place for excuse making. We're all here to win, right?"

The crowd erupted into a huge cheer, and Pearl began to wonder why she was even trying. She looked over the lake at Halinka, who was sitting glumly on the hill where she'd left her, and then over to Millie, who was still wriggling to try and get free. She knew they couldn't win, as Brains had been on board, which was against the rules, *and* she hadn't even made it across the lake. She picked up the tatty, old cat.

"Come on, Brains. It's okay. Let's make our way back around the lake and go rescue Millie and spend some time together, while we still

have some time left."

As she strolled along the water's edge, she listened to the awards-giving ceremony, and hot tears stung her eyes as Megan and Heather were named the winners of the competition. She watched as Nova Celeste handed them a beautiful trophy with silver rockets and golden stars wrapping around it.

"Everyone, please put your hands together as Megan and Heather fly a victory lap around the lake!" yelled the commentator.

"Pearl!" Millie shrieked as she jumped out from behind some bushes.

"Millie! How did you…?"

"Long story, but I had to resort to contortion. Did you see the Freezacon that flaked off Atom's craft and onto the lake surface? It was on fire!"

"Yes, yes, I did," Pearl said nervously. "They only just made it to dry land! If they do a victory lap, their craft will disintegrate completely and…"

Pearl and Millie looked over at Atom's craft. Megan and Heather were standing in front of it, busy arguing over who should do the victory lap.

Heather shoved Megan out of the way before clambering into the machine and pulling the helmet down over her head. But then Megan climbed on too.

"There's room for two," she seethed.

"Hey, ladies," the commentator said, shoving his microphone into Megan's face. "How does it feel to be the winners? Pretty awesome, huh?"

But Megan just pushed him away. "Let's go!" she snarled as she poked Heather in the ribs, and the craft begin to move.

"Oh no!" said Pearl.

Chapter 10

The crowd cheered wildly as Heather began making her way down the runway, picking up speed as she went.

"This can't be happening," Millie squeaked. "We have to do something."

"It's too late," Pearl said, watching helplessly.

Everything seemed to happen in slow motion. Pearl spun around and looked at all the cheering faces, then at Nova Celeste, jumping up and down in delight on the stage. She looked over to Halinka, who was packing away her things in

her bag and beginning to walk away from Lake Cosmos. How could this be happening? How had she let things get to this stage?

But as she turned around again, she noticed the expressions on the faces of people in the crowd had changed. They were no longer cheering—they were looking worried.

With a jolt, Pearl was back in real time. Megan and Heather's machine was still racing along the runway, but it was now violently shifting from side to side. She could just make out the students' voices. "Get off! Your bottom has over-loaded it!" Heather shrieked.

"No, you get off," Megan spat. "It's your bottom that's the problem."

But before either of them could blink, the flying machine seemed to hit something on the runway, sending both girls flying back away from the lake into the air. They landed on the giant bouncy castle while their flying machine carried on toward the lake at full pelt!

"Brains saved them!" cried Millie.

"Oh, well done, you clever, brave cat," Pearl said as she ran over to the runway to check he was still in one piece—or several pieces, at least. Apart from a lose back wheel and a dented head plate, he was fine.

"Pearl! Look out!" Millie shouted from farther back. Heather and Megan's flying machine was about to hit the water—and Pearl and Brains were too close.

"No!" Pearl shouted, trying to shield Brains from what was about to happen. There was a loud bang and a white flash. Pearl looked up quickly to see hundreds of tiny balls of white flame headed right for her and Brains. She closed her eyes. And then it was dark.

"Pearl? Pearl?" came a familiar voice. "Are you okay?"

"Halinka!" Pearl cried, throwing her arms around her friend and squashing Brains's ears in the process. "I thought you'd left. I thought you'd given up on me."

"Give up on you? No chance." Halinka smiled.

"Besides, you looked like you might be in need of that heatproof parasol you invented last semester, the one you thought was no good. I kept it after you threw it in the bin and have had it in my bag ever since." She gestured toward the large, umbrella-shaped dome that was protecting them from the heat of the explosion. "Turns out it's not only SPF 500 but Freezacon proof as well! I know an excellent invention when I see one."

Pearl smiled, a big tear running down her cheek. "So you do think I'm a good inventor?"

"Pearl, Halinka, Brains!" shrieked Millie as she arrived at the scene now that the flames had been put out. "Are you okay?"

"I think we're all just fine," Halinka said, helping Pearl to her feet. "Come on. Let's get out of here."

As the three friends put their arms around

one another, Brains in creaky pursuit, the loud-speaker crackled to life.

"Would Pearl Peppersmith, Millie Maranova, and Halinka Harrison please come up to the main stage?"

Chapter 11

The three young scientists nervously made their way around the lake to the stage area.

"I wonder what this is all about," Millie said anxiously, taking her glasses off to dry them,

causing her wet hair to stick to her face.

Halinka and Pearl giggled. "You look like a drowned squirrel," Halinka snorted.

Once they arrived, they were ushered behind a curtain to

one side, where they came face-to-face with Nova Celeste and two very guilty-looking Atom Academy girls.

"Ladies," Nova said, "it's a complete honor to meet you three. From what I can gather at this early stage, it seems you tried everything you could to warn Megan and Heather about the Freezacon they were using in their invention." She gestured over her shoulder to clipboard lady, who was looking much friendlier and a little regretful.

Nova turned to Megan and Heather. "I'm sorry, ladies, but you have been dis-qualified from the competition. I'll have to take that back."

She pried the

trophy out of Megan's grip and handed it to Pearl.

"Now, I think we need to redo the award-winners' ceremony, don't you? Would you help me?"

"Oh, we'd be totally honored," Pearl said. She knew they still wouldn't be the winners, but she was glad that the cheating Atom Girls had been stripped of their trophy.

Nova led the three Bunseners out onstage and stood before the confused crowd.

"Thank you all for your patience. Due to the enormous severity of what has just occurred, we have had no choice but to disqualify all of Atom Academy from the competition. So that means we must choose a new winner. Now I'm looking down my list here at the times and the second fastest crossing of Lake Cosmos was by...Sienna Selenium and Sophie Syntax

from Miss Bunsen's School for Brilliant Girls! Congratulations, ladies!"

Sienna and Sophie raced up onstage to claim their trophy. The crowd clapped and cheered, and all the Bunseners at the front threw hats and ties and shoes and squirrels up in the air.

"But that's not all!" Nova continued. "I have another special prize for some very deserving ladies."

She turned to face Pearl, Millie, and Halinka.

"You three girls are an example to young scientists and engineers of the future. You tried to warn Heather and Megan of the danger they were in, resulting in you losing your own machine. And you didn't let a squirrel-related setback stop you either; you rebuilt your machine with whatever you could find. That shows great ingenuity—something every scientist needs. And finally, you would have easily made it across the lake if it weren't for your overly helpful bionic cat. I, therefore, present to you an entire summer's stay at my Star Village Space Center. I guess we're going to be seeing a bit more of each other."

And at that, Nova Celeste gave them a cheeky wink and was ushered offstage by her security.

The five Bunsen girls all hugged, con-gratulating each other and listening as the rest

of the school roared the school name out loud: "Bunsen's, Bunsen's, Bunsen's!"

"I got to meet Nova Celeste, and I looked like a drowned squirrel." Millie sighed.

"We'll see you at Star Village!" Sienna said to Pearl as she and Sophie skipped off excitedly.

A second display of flying hats and hockey sticks and squirrels flew up in the air.

"Oh, you two," said Pearl. "I'm so happy we're all going to stay together this summer. I'm sorry my machine didn't work."

"It was *our* machine," said Millie.

"And it was really Brains's fault," Halinka chimed in. "Although he did do a grand job of saving Megan and Heather from a very toasty end!"

Pearl turned to her. "Thank you for giving up your Turbo Trike to keep us all together. I thought maybe you wanted to leave Miss Bunsen's and go to Velocity College after all."

"Oh, Pearl!" Halinka said, pulling her friend into a hug. "I would never want to leave Miss Bunsen's, and more importantly, I would never want to leave you. You're the best scientist I've ever known."

Pearl looked at her closely. "But Velocity College has all those great opportunities."

"Yes, but do they have squirrels?" Halinka said, laughing.

Pearl felt a rush of relief. She looked at Millie. "And thank you for cheering me on. I was beginning to think I wasn't good enough to be your friend."

"You are the best friend anyone could ever have!" Millie chided as she squeezed herself into the hug.

The three friends stepped down from the stage, ready to head home after their very exciting day.

"Hey, I think we could fix that machine and fly home!" said Halinka.

"Let's do it!" Pearl replied.

"Let's just do some calculations first," Millie protested, pulling a calculator out of her skirt pocket. But her plea went unheard as the sound of tools being unloaded from toolboxes rang out in the summer air.

Don't miss Pearl, Millie, and Halinka's first adventure!

HC ISBN: 978-0-8075-5157-8 (US $14.99)
PB ISBN: 978-0-8075-5154-7 (US $5.99)
e-Book ISBN: 978-0-8075-5156-1 (US $9.99)

Best friends Pearl, Millie, and Halinka love Miss Bunsen's School for Brilliant Girls, so they are horrified when they discover it may close down. Winning an interschool invention contest might give Miss Bunsen enough money to keep the school open, and Pearl, Millie, and Halinka are sure that their invention will take first place.

The Best of Yourself Hat gives the wearer confidence, a better vocabulary, and perfect hair. But it's such a good idea that a rival school steals their design! Can the friends find a way to save their invention...and their school?

Erica-Jane Waters lives in a tumbledown seventeenth-century cottage in deepest, darkest Northamptonshire, England, with her husband and two children, and their cats, George and Beatrix. She works from her attic studio and likes to discuss story ideas with the mice that live in the rafters above her writing desk. Much like Miss Bunsen's School for Brilliant Girls and its crumbling walls, her house requires an imaginative approach to everyday life, and, like the girls in her books, she loves coming up with inventive, make-do-and-mend design ideas to engineer a functional home!